# The Satanic Visions

## Rev. Joshua M. Escritt

iUniverse, Inc.
New York   Bloomington

# The Satanic Visions

*iUniverse books may be ordered through booksellers or by contacting:*

*iUniverse*
*1663 Liberty Drive*
*Bloomington, IN 47403*
*www.iuniverse.com*
*1-800-Authors (1-800-288-4677)*

*Because of the dynamic nature of the Internet, any Web addresses or links
contained in this book may have changed since publication and may no longer
be valid.*

*ISBN: 978-1-4502-1774-3 (sc)*
*ISBN: 978-1-4502-1775-0 (ebk)*

*Printed in the United States of America*

*iUniverse rev. date: 2/27/2010*

# Contents

# The Remedy

The imagination is the by-product of a persons' mind. It is produced from past memories that have been rearranged mixing with future thoughts. Our creativity is the memories next door neighbor. This stems from a persons' individuality. A persons incarceration happens because, of their own selves. Even though people are free from worldly prisons, they are still locked up on the inside and driven to insanity. For why, Generations have become accustomed to pain by living in it for so long. Many things drive people mad by the blindness of the human-animals' own mind. Many do not ever find true freedom. We've searched out looking for all the answers to feel better such as Religions, doctors, friends, and family. Yet no soothing answers. The key to freedom lay's within you. Search deep within because, you already have the answers to which you search for.

Memories came from past experiences and past experiences give us wisdom. We all learn at least one good lesson in life.

Our minds are the biggest libraries the world has to offer. Past experiences are triggered by people, places, smells, and sounds. Without these things we would have no clue to anything in life.

# Selling Your Soul

Simply the motion of giving yourself completely to your own carnal desires! There is no trading with this entity called Satan. The whole world is at your bidding, just go after it. Everything is already ours! Satan is a metaphorical representation of the beast in the heart of the Satanist.

# Heaven

Heaven is the other side of a person that brings balance to the hell side. Everything in a person's life is by their own choice. Heaven is in the world of flesh. By not causing pain and suffering to yourself. You can then say to yourself, I LOVE LIFE. Indulge in the things that please you and you shall live in joy.

# Abyss

Abyss is the state of nothingness. Abyss is complete black. Abyss is the stage of human death and there are no feelings or emotions.

# Lost in Confusion

(Thoughts from within)

Who are you? What injustice has my father committed against you?

He has forsaken his way with you Dark One.

Why have you come in his place and for what reason?

Because, I want to drink the blood of the Goat and gain life of joy through the deeds of my flesh! Will you honor me?

And why the talk of and concern for your father?

Well, he was my father, but his ways are of pain and sorrow. I no longer want to tread on the paths of pain. I want to be brought into temptation, strengthened, and filled with infernal forbidden delights.

Your selfish desires have made me well pleased.

I hath murdered my own brother in mine own beautifully jealous fit. I have shown my anger and I revel in it.

You now become Master Mahan!

Honor me that I may keep your image and teach me your laws, and that I may keep your precepts.

# A.M.K. Killer
## (Killer Poem)

Interrogations and suffering prophecies,

The violence within families and the corresponding realities!

The hatred burning inside and the psycho woman who caused the fall!

Blood no longer thicker than water!

Vengeance a way to relieve myself and prisons I no longer see.

Destroying a family by her lying tongue!

Crucified and inverted, her revelation perverted.

She has no good that will come of her.

Her only ability is the gift of a destructive nature.

She takes away a person's freedoms and real personalities.

These are the things she calls love.

She's a brutal sado-masochist of annihilation.

Her fucked up mentality and psychopathic raped brutality that destroys her lover in an instant.

So strong the snare that the other part of the configuration cannot completely break free!

Why does her presence still have to be?

Nothing of her is capable of speaking truth and showing love.

She is the truest definitive nature of evil, hypocritical with severe upheaval.

Her drug is a familiar chaos in formless matter and spiraling vortexes and still claims the definitive power of heaven and God.

Her own, ending lays near!

Self-destructing and annihilating power!

She is the current present evil and now banished from a once welcoming lair.

And, my curses to a psychopathic entity who shall never return!

Death and hatred is her blessing and may she vanish into heavens' foul and horrific vapors'.

A dirty whore of iniquity!

# Satanic Brother
## (Poem)

Spiraling down, down, down!

I have raised myself up in strength to stand my ground.

From the error of a misplaced trust!

I've abandoned my friend for the new drug lust.

I've called out to the world, that my voice be heard by
my brother.

I've made some mistakes and I'm sure you already knew.

Separated by incarceration because of Satanic Sin!

YES, we have rules that govern within.

A brighter future will surely hold true.

Brother, hold on, I know all seems lost, I will catch up
no matter the cost.

Followed by thought!

Against the holy light I fought.

Concern in vain!

All those churches I set aflame.

Brought on by Christians own slander.

And, so we fought for satanic plunders.

Brother, hold on, I know all seems lost, I will catch up
no matter the cost.

I'm almost free to search for thee!

In the night with whirlwind flight!

The demon's we trust to unite us.

Our indulgence in sin is the devils' delight.

The bonding with Hell is our Heaven.

And, their bonding with Heaven is their Hell.

As I passed through the flame, I'd been given a name.

I am the demon that's been sent back to earth.

To enjoy my next task of fleshly deserts!

Brother, hold on, I know all seems lost, I will catch up no matter the cost.

I am here with the flames of Hell burning strong and black.

With hatred and killing, the murderous attack.

There's no end, never was any beginning. HA!

I'm ALL and Everything.

It's all just illusions'.

A life of infernal bliss!

I'm standing in a place where time can not exist.

# Blood Lust Peace
# (Song)

I have given you this great poison.

From the great black sky!

If, you'll surely drink it in!

You'll begin to enjoy this life.

From where all creation has sprung forth,

Where Lucifer abides!

Enchanted by the frenzied beast!

Roaring, howling, from the east!

Drank from the goblet of Blood Lust Peace!

Then comes union rooted with sin!

Darkness grabs hold deep within!

Six hundred soldiers sent by Satan!

With sixty priest to enforce creation!

Six standing wizards who cast their spells!

To conquer Heaven and send Christ to Hell!

Enchanted by the frenzied beast!

Roaring, howling, from the east!

Drank from the goblet of Blood Lust Peace!

Entered through the proclamation!

By desecration and fornication!

Adoration under one Satanic Nation!

Enchanted by the frenzied beast!

Who sat me down for the devils feast!

Severed the heads of the lambs of god!

I showed them what their slander cost.

Through all these cycling's of ages and times,

Why have these not been Christian crimes?

Enchanted by the frenzied beast!

Roaring, howling, from the east!

I've drank from the goblet of Blood Lust Peace.

# Carpe Noctem
## (Poem)

Infernal One, hast thou come?

Ever envelope my being with thy cloth pitch black.

All around me the fires burn tormenting those without!

I sit on my throne!

In darkness I reign!

Welcome, I greet you!

Not turning back from this path!

I have granted your heart's desire!

Honor me and I will you!

A while you wait for me in the abyss!

Dense darkness of inspiration ensue me!

9 purify with black flame, provide me!

Open doors unto my remembrance!

So, that the field bloody shall know your vision!

I granted your request!

Hear my command, you splendid-delightful-stimulating-infernally black eyes, with fires of Hell to light my path!

Your left hand I am given.

Your right hand things are taken.

Open wide! Blast forth!

Hounds break the barriers and flood circle of habitat!

I am One and the same as you.

Splendidly and infernally stout!

You have given me the sign in the west high!

Sky blood red so.

Hold back no more!

We ride together.

Hail Satan! Hail Satan! Hail Satan!

I am He!

You have aligned yourself with me.

GO!

You now hold the power over the kingdom.

All shall go forth at your bidding.

Commanding Legions!

Serpent Religions!

Hail Black!

Strike and attack!

Center thy deep!

Enter thy sleep!

Forever they weep.

Reverenced amongst men!

The driving within!

Satan on high!

Ruling the sky!

Christians of past and murdering the last!

Satanic Revelry! Satanic Revelry! Satanic Revelry!

# The Foothold

A few who are strong is better than a million weak. For, the strong will conquer and rule the continuance of the flesh. The flesh will die, and as the memory will stand sure. I stand forth as a king who protects his army and land. OH' the war, fearing not death! Death has welcomed me, when it is due. Side with me and enter the kingdom for I have spoken. My One command is the Loyalty to our honored Ancestors'. Stand up in battle and win the war.

# The Four You Came
# (Poem)

The fiery plane, driving insane!

The people of old, covered in mold.

The fiery Hell and dead body smell!

The rotting of Christ!

We killed off the lies.

Into the past, remolding the cast!

Ancient cries of the gods' in the skies!

Murdered Christians and burned paradise.

The One last adventure!

Into the ocean blue tincture!

Leviathan has risen!

From the blue sea of reason!

O' lasting curse!

She drove the hearse with dead bodies dispersed.

The moist and fertile whore!

We broke open Hell's door.

The country of blood and land of war!

My desires I cannot help,

I only want more.

Impregnated by sky,

Born of air!

All-powerful you cannot snare.

And, the captivating breath of knowing what's left!

The creation of four things made you the god of war.

Inspiration!

The mesmerization!

Into Darkness,

Our Satanic Nation!

Vobiscum Salve. Vobiscum Salve.

Salve! Salve! Salve!

# I Am Samael

For those who don't know I am not friendly, unless you're blood bound to me. Bonded by oath and symbolized goat, I am vengeful and unrelenting. I hate you and all that you are. If, you oppose me, then horrible unimaginable death will befall your whole bloodline. Your kin will cease to exist. My gift to you, call it extinction!

I will tear apart your flesh, just give me that test. I know what's best in darkness I judge. Thy mystery of me you seek. If you shall find, then you already lost your life. Maybe alive, but, now I own your soul and there's no turning back. Think well before approaching me, lest you regret ever meeting me, for your life may be lost or great agony for the years to be.

I am rampant wrath and chaos is my delight! Unto you, you may win my favor and for me just your soul. Do as I say. I as you command. Unto you, your request is granted. So, my beloved brother, favor in my eyes you have won. And, you are being dedicated to the bloodshed of those who would speak vile against you. As it would be spoken against me also!

I am favored and in this life I am one, unto you the driving life force in me. Forever Samaels' Requiem! You know who I am don't you? Yea! Woe! Yea! Woe! Woe, Woe! Enter now _____ Never, coming back. Well Pleased _____.

# Devil Baby Sonata in Black (My Anthem)

I lift you up, above thy creation.

Infernal Lord, my life well spent.

You promised me, thy worldly blessings.

Thy fulfillment of my flesh the joys of life are what I love best.

Infernal Majesty above all else!

I've lived my life with no regrets.

My love to Lord Lucifer I hath shown to fit.

By indulging self into my own carnal desires,

And for thy flames of Hell burneth bright.

From the depths of Hell I call tonight.

My heart is set aflame, with mine own desires.

The kingdom shall reign for all eternity.

So, bring your light to help me shine.

I am the hyper star,

The world is mine.

I lift you up, above thy creation.

Infernal Lord, my life well spent.

You promised me, thy worldly blessings.

The fulfillment of my flesh,

The joys of life are what I love best.

Infernal Majesty above all else!

I lift you up, above thy creation.

Infernal Lord, my life well spent.

Long live your beauty!

Hail Satan!

# South Invocation

Thee I invoke, nameless serpents, guardians of desirous lust from the bottomless pit of Hell, the gate of ineffable life!

Do, thou stand at my side!

In the names of Mantus and Mania, God and Goddess of Hell, the pentagram, do, thou stand firm next to me!

Against Christ the voices of righteousness, do, thou stand firm!

Be thou the eyes next to me,

The fire next to me,

The sword in my hand,

The spear of shibboleth against thy holy,

And thy armor that clothes me!

Be guarding and watching, Daemons of the Southern reaches,

Remember your people!

# East Invocation

Thee I invoke, Mistress, Goddess of night, Metztli, Queen of Dark Magic, Proserpine, of the underworld and the heights of Kali!

Thee I call forth this night to guard and protect this sacred rite against the twelve apostles and their holiness, the true Evil Maskim, the true Lords of the vilest evil!

Thee I summon, Mistress, Goddess of night, Metztli, Queen of Dark Magic, Proserpine, of the underworld and the heights of Kali, that thou may protect and guard us from the eyes of the righteous and the vile ways, and the poison of the righteous, striking Christ god!

Be guarding and watching, Daemons of the Eastern Winds and remember! Daemons of the East, Remember your people!

# North Invocation

Thee I invoke, Ishtar, Silver hunter, from Babylon the fertile Earth I summon.

Thee I call forth to guard and protect the northern hemisphere of the most sacred rite against the vicious Muslim terrorist who would destroy all that is true and just accordingly to the laws of this nature.

Be thou most vigilant and brutal against the encouragers of false hope and their suicidal death threat!

Hail to the Throne of Azag-Thoth!

Bring thy poison on thy fiends of Iraq!

Bring thy wrath before the Syrian fiends!

Bring thy weapons upon the fiends of Allah!

Heave your wrath upon those hordes of Angels of Islam and their people, in all ways and on all sides, and all places of their living!

Be guarding and watching, Daemons of the Northern hemisphere!

Remember us, Infernal One, King of our Homeland, Victory of every war and conqueror over every one of our adversaries.

See our lights and hear our heralds, and do not forsake us.

Daemons of the North, Remember your people!

# West Invocation

Thee I invoke, Dagon of the Philistine Waters!

Thee I invoke, Mephistopheles to cast away life!

From the unknown Darkness, shall you serve me!

To thee unknown Daemon, shall you serve me!

From the unknown enemy, shall you defend me on all sides!

To the unknown sorcery, you shall teach me!

From the wrath of those without, you shall keep me!

From false acquisitions by the sanctified lies that they without consider privileged, you shall keep me from!

From any who seek my ending, you shall keep me from!

Be guarding and watchful, Daemons of the Western Waters,

And, remember your children!

# Third Dimension
# (Song)

I lifted the veil and a burst of energy to open the gates.

I sprang from the deep.

Entered the 5 and 9!

I sent my spell in time.

Those of Ancient past,

Rise up strong and fast.

The new cycle is vast.

I slaughtered the holy path.

Spilling their blood with sword from Azazel!

The third dimension! The third dimension!

Unknown mystery, present in the darkness!

The memory of past virtue!

It is the understanding that I seek.

I can know all I am all!

From darkness black,

From abyss came comfort,

And, to self purification of the flame so black!

From whence came Hell!

The third dimension! The third dimension!

Spilling Christian blood with Azazels' sword!

The rebound of wondrous delights!

Mysteriously posed in night,

And the ornamented presentation of black hooded
robes!

The eyes are raging with fire,

His heart a beast!

The paralyzation of yet another world!

I crept through the gates by transformation.

A different mask and a different figure!

I've changed a new shape!

With the poignant smells that linger,

Incensum cordum!

The third dimension!

# Dark Father Adoration

Hail to the Dark Father who hath concealed well his form. Yet, hath revealed your nature unto me! Vast and dark is your dwelling! I have come to lift the veil to your mystery! Infernal creator of this world of horror, I've represented your being to thy fullest. In turn manifesting your worldly embrace! Together what may to strike down my adversaries with your impending doom!

The serpents of the first flame show a sign of supreme wisdom! O' your calling, your glorious and mysterious form out of the night! Your great black wings, hath covered me with thy infernal love and protection, guiding my every step in the path I've vowed. Sustain me, o' great sustainer, for only you have the unconquerable power which exceeds beyond all eternity.

My Infernal King and Majesty, Dark and Mysteriously Splendidly in motion, Father of men, The God of all gods', Lord Satan to you it be, my honor and recognition for the years to come. Walking only in thy illumination of your black flame from Hell! Intelligence and intellect you've given me and your wonders will last for centuries to come! Only through you Dark One does thy World of Horror stay in perpetual motion.

# Dark Mother Adoration

Hail to thee, Hecate the Dark Mother!

Dark Mother of mystery who hath aided me in all your doings! I do honor to your name that my life of indulgence to passion darkly and mine vengeance only through you. Dark expression of thy image to my successful completion which carry on your works that shall manifest your glory Infernal on earth! O' Dark Mother whose time be endless and darkly splendid in the depths of Hell. You have come by night to aid me in mine time of need. I recognize and honor your name and proudly proclaim thee unto all ages in the World of Horror. Despite the consequence of charged punishments on those scrolls, I stand faithfully by your side. I fear not any who try and stand in my way. For you shall strike them down in that moment they even attempt to plot my destruction. My dark expression of emotions of love and of compassion to you, and in turn you have granted me strength to endure. I hath given myself to you, O' Hecate, hear your son Dark Mother!

# Embracing Life
# (Poem)

Ritual's of old locked in my mind.

Ceremonies of sacrifice, looking at time!

Attitudes and beliefs within us all,

Masquerading with hatred,

The summoning from Hell!

Nights' are stimulating and the secrets we never tell,

All those screams from the incinerated Christian shell.

Calling out to their God,

We've condemned him to Hell.

We've taken over his realm with violence,

They've been shamed,

And we slaughtered their prophets,

The Satanic Hall of Fame!

Knowing our future a darkness within,

I've realized this night where I've truly been.

I hold on to everything,

I have ever learn to know,

This time has come to find my path and the only way
that's true.

Visions of thy Baphomet,

In a night storm,

On a mountain with Satan,

With a concern that is now in vain.

The conduct of becoming tried,

In the Dark Lords' realm where I abide!

All my life has been dear and true,

In the light of Lucifer everything is new.

The time has come,

He wants his due.

"The beast within us glorifies itself into the manifestations of the worldly embrace."

# One Chance
## (Poem)

In the time of a dying friend,

Everything's been lost.

Where do I begin?

The times we shared,

The memories well kept.

If, I had one more night with him!

Surely, it would be luck!

The pain of missing him so badly,

A horrible tragedy!

My heart full of sorrow!

I begin seeking vengeance,

For the murder of my brother,

And I was granted another continuance.

# SyLaBoL
## (Song)

Humans come and humans go,

Jesus died so let him go.

Centuries have wept at their defeat.

Lucifer here and Hecate there,

Satan will meet you anywhere.

He's in your heart and in your head,

Slaughtering those lambs that bled blood red,

Symbolical Christians all dropped dead.

The tearing and screaming and yearning,

Because Satan's hatred is burning,

Against Christian and Muslim learning!

Broke open wide the dreadful minions,

Sprang forth demonic children!

I've pierced the veil of night,

I've ratified and renewed my right.

And my flesh is moved by the four cardinal points.

# Dark Father Invocation

In the name of the Dark Father exalted above and below, hear me this night. Let all your fantasies manifest in the darkest world and in the minds of all those who would pursue your assistance. Do not turn from us, I command you! Give ear unto my calling! Let all the whirlwinds of Hell rage fiercely without mercy!

Let all the earth tremble at your coming, let all the lightning strike with vengeance unto your glory on our adversaries who would oppose us, let the thunders sound your mighty name so that all may know your ruler-ship of the world of flesh and blood, let the fires from Hell burn away all hypocritical corruption off this earth so that the freedoms of Satanic thought have not any more plagues.

Rise up from the depths of Hell to manifest my desires.

Hail Satan!

# Dark Mother Invocation

Thy Dark Mothers name I have spoken.

By my command, you have responded.

You have heard thy words of _____ from thy heart of flesh where your blood hath journeyed endlessly.

Hecate is your name and boldly I speak the infernal sounds of Hell to call out into your domain.

Hear my summoning of need this hour and night! Your undefiled knowledge of enlightenment I invoke. I shall not let you rest until you've answered my need. Let it be that your presence be my life-long companion and that we shall become one. For I fear not your power. Your dark nature and divine energy is in accordance to my will. Let it be that your name in itself be a protection shield of infernally black radiance.

By fire I command thee that you shall come into agreement with my desires.

By air you have caused the life force of human-animals.

By earth your mother aspect has granted me thy blessings of worldly delights.

By water you're constant change of the higher role in advancement of individuality and creativity.

I have assumed many forms that I myself am a mysterious vapor.

Hail to the Dark Mother!

# I'm God
# (Poem)

Why must I be questioned?

My authority is above all!

They entered their suffering for two centuries weeping.

Die Christianity by your own self defeating.

You've walked through this life with your slander and strife,

Attempting to tear down the satanic life!

Fear me, hear me, and bow down before me.

Fear me, hear me, and bow down before me.

Killing off of all what's left.

Murdering Christians by these conjuring riffs!

The weapons I have tested.

Wearing blood stained vests.

Closing in on my vengeance within,

Burning my enemy with sardonic grin!

Fear me, hear me, and bow down before me.

Fear me, hear me, and bow down before me.

I'M GOD! I'M GOD!

Hail Satan.

It's my victory I win.

# The Thirty Silver (Poem)

I plunged into the deep dark, black pit of Hell.

I swooped up the governed thirty pieces of silver.

From a piece to another piece I was surely led to another piece.

I gained the worldly power,

I became the king of Hell.

From my thoughts I sent forth into the darkly splendid Abyss.

I transformed all that is.

Why have I been questioned?

Why the blame of me for your failures?

Is it not, your own fault for the lack of your own knowledge?

Is it not, the beginning of your own un-wisdom?

I have granted you all earthly success.

Instead, you have soiled your own being by error and delusion.

AWAKEN! My children!

This is the Satanic Age!

Understand me and my creation.

# Blasphemies
## (Song)

I have not fallen from grace,
I have destroyed the holy place,
No more Christians or Jewish race.
I've come to condemn that race!
Blasphemies! Ancient Blasphemies!
Forsaken not this life of flesh,
The dark gods kill the rest.
Ancient Blasphemies!
I've murdered thy holy host,
Denied the Holy Ghost!
Blasphemies! Ancient Blasphemies!
I pissed on the prophets of heaven,
And crushed their holy name!
I'm the first spawn of the black flame.
Blasphemies! Ancient Blasphemies!
The teachings of yet a cowardly way,
The self-denial and blind faith!
They hide behind their holy cross.
And just like the winds they are thrown and tossed.
Ancient Blasphemies………………………………..

# Black Star God (Poem)

They've called me,

By the blackest star,

In the night sky!

Are you ready?

For the Christian death!

I HAVE COME!

What you seek, answer to me.

You're already granted.

For the price of your soul!

Black star god rise up for me!

Black star god with flames of Hell!

I've obeyed thy teachings,

And thy commandments well kept.

Oh' HEAR THE LAW!

I'm now transformed!

I'm god!

Hearts been fueled and set ablaze!

By four elements I command!

Flame of comfort which I desire!

Black star god rise up for me.

Black star god with flames of Hell!

Black Star God.....

Creative brain,

Whose image is insane!

Rejoice NOW for Satan's reign!

They will call me,

By the blackest star in the night!

# SZANDOR

Teacher of the arts,

Father of the way,

Hast thou come to show me?

The left hand blessing trade!

In the east I look,

For a daily sign of thee!

As in the west I've served thee best,

With altars and rituals nigh!

Your humor must have been a powerful joy,

To hear your voice and shake your hand!

As if I met the cheerful heart,

And only then, will I, know where to start.

A man of honor, a man of integrity,

A man of strength and forbidden fruits and with
answers to life!

The only one who revealed the truth to my presence!

And set me on my way.

Teacher of the arts and father of the way,

Hast thou come to guide me?

Through the left hand blessing trade!

# Freedom through Passage

Out of the night I come to you!

Out of the night I call to you!

Hear my voice of infernal delight!

I gave you all, your rightful plight.

Striking distance, vengeance assured,

Rivers of blood and earth concurred.

Set the law of Satanic thought,

My evil mind begins to plot.

To destroy Christians and heaven too,

Don't forget Muslims and the Jews.

Leave none standing for their crimes,

Of slander, of theft, of shifting blame,

And their commitment of murder,

By burning our ancestors in the flame!

For our freedoms of creative thought,

Individuality is now safely sought.

Without the fear of their punishments of death by fire,

And innocent loss a murder for hire.

I command Satan's spawn to rise up in time,

With strength and war and daemonic rhyme!

I've offered up the sacrifice!

Incensed with Dragons Blood and Black Opium twice!

Light the candles and watch them burn,

And project thy image strong and thrice.

Commander of earth and of Hell,

I've conjured you to assist in thy infernal spell.

Commanding fire burning fierce,

Commanding air to cause thy birth!

Commanding earth of great foundation,

And unto thy raging sea,

The thanks to creation!

Rise up fast, rise up strong!

I resurrected Satan into flesh,

Alive for an eternity, eternally long!

Out of the night I come to you!

Out of the night I call to you!

Set the law of Satanic thought,

My evil mind begins to plot.

Hear my voice of infernal delight,

I'll show you all, your rightful plight.

Freedom through passage!

# Stupidity of Validity

The blue dope gave me false hope,

I resurrected that old rugged cloak.

This shit has been no joke,

And it's made my eyes float.

The venom in the needle,

I was given the shared life of a beetle.

Empty and so dark,

From all this crazy time apart!

Have yet seen the spark to ignite that fire,

For my heart to have that yearning desire!

To quit the game of self deceit,

My enslavement shall be my defeat.

Sobered up to figure out,

All my problems with no doubt!

Only to find out deep within,

That's all I want: that shit again.

That shit is killing me so,

And, this I truly know.

Why, must I leave this life?

Enslaved to that dope!

It made me feel complete and truly set free,

It's just the illusions caught up in me,

That was all I could see.

Could it be a number one sin rooted in me?

There has been only one enemy,

Man with his law to dictate my well-being.

I know the shame of that cost,

For all my memories I do not want lost.

The awesome times I had,

In the country on some abandoned land,

With my friend who made me surely so glad.

My friend has been gone and left me so sad,

I'm left alone to carry on that tradition that we once
had.

We took new adventures out of town,

We looked for Annie to bring back around.

All for the love of the drug!

Jeff's a generous man with awesome heart,

Some punk ass kid ruined it,

With a bullet through the heart!

My hatred rages with fierce pain!

Our wonderful memories of watching it snow,

Through the looking glass,

We see our crystalline ho.

Off to the casino to celebrate,

And many girls to fornicate!

(In loving memory: Jeffrey Carl Steppuhn 1979-2005)

# Message of Old

Shape-shifters dancing their spiral madness!

Haunting every angle in yet another image, the calling of darkness in the hearts of those who dare to walk with the undead and talk to the dead. Hearing the voices of another world and yet still advancing the dark abyss.

In time they will come, creeping through any opening they can find. Through the channels of the mind you have no warning. Once you enter there is no return. Come! Come! Rise up out of the bottomless pit and show yourselves! Every Satanic ancestor of mine, hear me!

As the infernal vampires rose up and walked the big city streets at night, they filled their bellies with blood. Their carefully chosen victims they stalked with swift movement.

Werewolves intruding out of the wooded land to feast on human flesh, they cleaned up the lifeless mess of bodies the vampires left behind. There's no redemption for past action. Only to find yourself playing the game of life! It is self-preservation! Will you survive?

# Veil of Satanic Passage

All the fortified cities they say are indestructible! Hence, came that day the sulfurous flames burned fierce and wiped away all that could ever be possible to imagine. The pains of creation to yet be destroyed!

For why, I ask myself? Could it be that the gods hath become very angry? Or shall the wise man evade punishment by understanding the ways of the world? To deny oneself, does that make him any greater? Or, will the misery itself be greater of the process of forsaking your own life?

When the moon explodes into many pieces and the blood that drips off of them fills the earth that replace all water supply, shall we then thirst from the bloodied virgin? Why hast, not any path been success when there is only one ending to all stories?

To fulfill my skin hath become a blessing in another disguise, enjoying our goblets of red water drink. Shemhamforash!

Sufferings toil around and cling to the hearts of hypocritical indulgences.

Then, to ask the point of being forgiven or is it a game of how many sins I can deposit in the bank before I die? It's called direct deposit. If someone supposedly paid some price for my sins or everyone's sins, then, we better get every single penny worthwhile since the devil is on our side. Shemhamforash!

# Sorrow

Once upon in the distance;

I saw a demon hung.

For doing a small act of kindness,

For a horrible job un-done!

I saw a tear fall from his eye,

And a drop of blood the big surprise.

Why hast thou been weeping?

I asked him and he said,

"For two-thousand years, they still are searching."

Yet they have not found or going to find,

That heart of gold, its turned silver this time.

Artificial implants,

And the development of artificial human companions,

The only ones who understand,

And the only ones I champion.

Seek the truth by questioning,

And wisdom you shall gain.

In the light of truth, it's been believed that they are all
lies.

The devil knows best,

Why ask why?

# I Love You Satan

Come to me! Oh' god of infernal beauty!
I pay homage to your name and all your glory.
Shemhamforash!
My soul has been refined forever!
In Satan's name Jesus has to flee from me.
That's why I love you Satan!
I love you Satan more than life in the heavens!
I love you Satan for you're my life's true worth.
Satan ascended from Hell,
By the infernal messiah, Lucifer!
He came to indulge my life,
And his love endures forever,
And the lust for someone's lover!
Because of this I shall not turn away from him!
I love you Satan more than life in the heavens!
I love you Satan for you're my life's true worth.
Come to me! Oh' god of infernal beauty!
I pay homage to your name and all your infernal glory.

# The Pact

The falling rain and beating pain,

Dreaming the vain and curious for fame!

Vanity and desperation,

Obedient in desolation!

Seek and you find,

The next riddle to a murderous crime!

Why all the pain?

An operation has gone insane.

It is my comfort to feel alive,

And without the growing pains of knowledge,

My life will stop as like death.

Venom from the serpent,

And plenty to share,

Shredding my skin I burst in a flare.

Sailed off into the lake of fire,

In a brimstone boat,

For another funeral empire!

Seeking the devil,

He showed you his grin,

For if you truly knew,

That your life surely begins.

Symbolized goat,

I avoid cutting mans throat.

Finger in blood I have made my pact for good.

# Trading Places

Blood bound you said!

Who am I to question?

I'm not a doctor or a lawyer!

Yes, I can negotiate,

My soul for yours!

The devil laughed.

He's joking!

Step right up.

Done deal!

Yea!

Energy crashes by lightening,

And the thunder strikes.

I'm in for a ride shall I say?

The journey of walking in another's shoes!

I rose to power in the darkest hour,

We opened the gates of hell,

To make Christians cower.

That is the power that exceeds me now.

In trading places!

# Doctor of Darkness

Founded by a friend,

Conquered with a grin!

Satisfaction of life's contentment,

Astral projected yet to another planet.

The bargain of Mars,

And the pleasure of Venus!

Trapped inside by the mixture of both!

Don't know which way to go!

What witch?

Sending love!

No, war!

Misconceived by Fridays luck!

Deified by Tuesdays trust!

Set aflame he hast thou said!

A friend,

Who brought the trust and sacred truth in!

Never ending infernal glory,

As we watch him in the sky.

Aurora Borealis passes by!

He built the church with a wonderful fragrance,

As he founded and structured the bold amazement!

He's still my friend!

Infernal love always!

# Caught in the Twilight

Caught in the twilight,

Of yet even more gods',

Expressing their duties where human destinies lay.

The bitter cold of darkness,

And the shredded holy practice.

It's freezing down here!

Someone lied!

They said I would burn!

Even the black flame is not hot.

It is only purifying me.

What in the hell?

Let me try again!

Will I be granted another appearance?

To reach my new flesh for my next continuance!

Daemonic work that's what it's called!

I'm still caught in the twilight.

# My Blessing

One day the never ending black will find me!

I search and he gives me power.

Chaos and love blended together,

And not insanities as the Christians believe.

I'm purely sane,

The rest of the world is screwed up.

I see the hidden truths!

I'm a Satanist!

What else in this screwed world would I want be?

Sure in the hell not a Jesus baby!

Although he did practiced some mighty find
necromancy and levitation in his time.

I'm given the world!

What do you have?

False hope, you call that something?

It's a bunch of shit!

I can pull a roaring lion out my hat,

And at least a belief in something rather than nothing!

The devil has always been a lust object.

Can't you see?

He set me free!

# In The Gloom

Grey clouds show their intent,
And darkness where life grows!
The grey clouds burdens,
Give growth for certain.
Plants and trees need the burden of cloud tears,
And that the grey clouds carry.
The gloom of day brings sunshine later.
Will the empire of beauty appear?
In the pale silver moon light,
The blood is shed.
For the soldiers in my war are,
Avatars that only want more!
Sprinkled with this,
And sprinkled with that,
We cut the tongue of a virgin cat.
We sent them sailing off,
Because of the master plan of Satan's combat!
Call it sorcery!

# Defiled Virgins

Virgins of God our holy prey,

Tearing down heaven to find where they stay.

The demons shall blast forth like the raging winds!

A blood thirst storm for a virgin sacrifice!

Ravaging daughters of the Lamb of God,

Vile anger demented and condemned by the rod.

The savage brutal host,

A puritanical roast,

Of dead body virgins of Christianities most.

I, Satan's warrior command these things to be!

Upon the whirling fire, on high I ride.

My kingdom is filled with legions of black hoardes,

And defiled nuns cast out by the church.

Defiled virgins of infinite bliss,

Discarded Jesus for Satan's kiss!

Defiled virgins of infinite bliss,

To indulge in the poison,

The darkness that is!

Those who are unwilling to submit to the south of command,

I shall burn with thy fire to bury in sand.

Defiled virgins of infinite bliss,

Discarded Jesus for Satan's kiss!

Defiled virgins of infinite bliss,

To indulge in the poison,

The darkness that is!

# Fire

The burning flame of multipurpose,

Show yourself to me.

Will you come and be my light?

And, to shine forth Lucifer in this night!

The flames of desire,

Loves empire!

Guiding me through every spell,

And opened the gates of down south, called Hell!

Satan's indulgence of lust called love,

True to the name of the envious dove!

The raining fire in the Satanic Empire,

I've called the south, the flame of desire.

Hear me black flame!

My heart aflame for Satan's fame!

I cast down Christ and his holy shame.

# East Air

I entreat you O' Lucifer,

To Frankincense and Myrrh!

I bathe you in splendor,

I'm infernally yours!

Hear me Lucifer I invoke thee this night.

For love lust life,

For a newly wed wife,

Give unto me a satanic life.

Lucifer, O' Lucifer,

Mighty in splendor!

Come to me O' shinning one,

For this ritual has just begun.

With shouting and singing and merry drink,

I fall in love with the new satanic link.

Spawn thy children with breath of life,

With your air all around to rid my strife,

I have new satanic children and a wife.

Thanks to you East Air.

# West Water

You've given me thy gift of inspiration,

Blessed be thy satanic nation.

Creativity is part of me,

Left deep inside for eternity!

Eternally!

Blood is water of Leviathan,

Make me many like the sand.

Internally, infernally!

Hear me gods I call thee!

From deep within the heart,

Make my life on a whole new start.

I'm part of you and you part of me,

With thousands of blessings,

And children and wife and new life for me!

# Love Carries On

A love so strong and kin to the spirit,

Can only rest without fear in it!

Why the departing of a love that was so true?

When this magical moment is all I knew.

Peace to you for strength has been great,

It's time we parted do to fate.

Disagreements always get in the way,

But, my love will surely stay.

Only in this night,

I've served this life with beautiful plight.

Can the love endure even after we're apart?

Love all over in the next world part.

Until I am given to another royalty,

And give birth to the magical child born with loyalty.

To keep our heritage strong,

We share the love for all the years long.

# North Earth

Strength, you're my strength!

You are my foundation upon where I build a dark nation.

My love and gratefulness and respect I show.

For my life becomes successful this I know.

I owe you all of myself for an eternity,

With all honor and dignity!

Blessed be, I offer a gift,

Of incense and laughter for the law of thrift!

Blessed be, my queen mother earth.

I will surely show you my life's true worth.

Blessed be the earth,

Blessed be the trees,

Blessed be the fertile soil,

Blessed be the life giving beauty.

# Electric Chair Vomit

Energy and synergy to unite me with Hell!

The power of your bondage,

The dead body shell.

The shock to the heart,

Three worlds apart and life's spent looking for answers,

I found them in the black arts.

Hail Satan!

Revenge on the Christians,

For all duration!

Electric chair vomit!

Into the chair where I strap you in there,

It has to be the bondage I swear.

Taking lives while it comes to life,

The energy sent through the foul smelling chair.

Looking for answers through the practice of the black
arts,

The chair only sent me three worlds apart.

Electric chair vomit!

From the chair the vomit of the dead,

The shocking experience that conquers you dead!

A painless ending of the story you read!

Electric chair vomit, electric chair vomit!

Another realm that we build because we hated,

Their paradise of sorrows and torments sublime,

We built this chair for their Christian crime.

We called it electric chair vomit.

They created their hell for their spirit to yell,

And we created the chair for their bodies shell.

A flip of the switch and the surge was sent,

To paralyze their souls and tormented joy!

The demons come running to the sound of the scream,

To drag them down with their hypocritical regime!

Electric chair vomit is all we got.

Electric chair vomit for its life we fought.

Electric chair vomit, our victory we sought.

# In The Dark

Satan's coming in the night,
Serpent wings the beast has been struck.
Into darkness on leathern wings,
Satan's victory the slavery defeat!
Fortified and sent into the night.
Visions conquered and laid to rest.
All hail Satan.
In the dark,
Light of spark,
The black flame and Valhalla aflame!
In the dark!
In the dark!
For my spirit, shall descend to hell,
All this darkness,
The screams and yells and calling to the holy one,
You're condemned to hell.
In the dark, my brothers in blood,
We conquer with Voodoo,
We should, we should!
Where have you gone?
I've been awaiting thee!
Why have you come?
Searching for lost souls,

For the kingdom of hell!

I have not forsaken you or the demons spell,

In the dark I have risen from hell,

Orders from my god,

Satan I hail!

Always our battle in the dark,

All the demons chanting in the dark!

The celebrations of sulfur and fire,

In the dark, in the dark!

Hot winds inside, so I lift my veil,

For what it's worth you fucking nutshell!

In the dark the angels are weeping,

Because of their tattered wings,

From their own self defeating.

Die Christianity, your lambs are bleeding.

In the dark is where I dwell,

I pray for the demons to be released from hell.

In the dark my peace returns to me,

All my joys I've been blessed infernally.

Satan rise up out of the dark,

I command you spirit!

Your life I impart and forever I dwell in the dark.

Hail Satan.

# Cemetery

Out I go walking to a place that's my home,

It's midnight so I have begun,

The digging six feet down.

It's the corpse I want!

What do you think I am?

I'm a fucking Necromancer!

In this cemetery where I raise the dead!

They tell me so much and about the warriors death.

Many, many secrets,

They have given me well!

The death of all it comes at midnight.

Demons and angels, they fight for their plight.

In the cemetery where the real things exist!

The passions of remembrance,

My ancestors rest!

I walk through the isles of the 1600's,

I found three witches,

I raised them up and set them free,

I did it all, because of me.

The peace, the love, there is no pain!

The joy of the dead,

They prophecy the shame!

Return back to me this I command,

Obey my authority by the powers of hell!

I conquered you and sent you to hell.

Cemetery!

In the cemetery where life reforms,

It's the place I surely adorn.

In the cemetery I dwell.

# Bloodied Angels

The war in heaven fell to earth,

For Satan's vengeance, satanic rebirth!

The spawn of first flame,

With lustful shame!

Bloodied angels my revenge is on god!

Bloodied angels I rule with my rod.

They were all from the choir,

Satanic music they play!

They were cast down and tattered their wings,

Ceremonies of opposite, these demons they sing.

Bloodied angels my revenge is on god!

Bloodied angels I rule with my rod.

They rise to the battle with their wings spread wide,

They were sent from up above for the murder of holy lives.

Cast away light for darkness to come,

Off to the march for our game is redrum.

Bloodied angels my revenge is on god!

Bloodied angels I rule with my rod.

The war in heaven fell to earth,

For Satan's vengeance a satanic rebirth!

Bloodied angels my revenge is on god!

Bloodied angels I rule with my rod.

Bloodied angels -------------- The fucking bloodied
angels.

# Phallic Symbol

I fucking raped you impaled Christ!
I murdered the virgin and cursed you thrice.
Holy defilement and the virgin's sacrament,
Fucking Catholics!
I have your aspergent,
The phallic symbol for blessing thy way,
And for my blasphemies:
It's all murder to clear my way,
The masculine power and of Satan this night!
This phallic symbol for rituals that draw nigh!
Phallic treasure to safe guard the night,
And the power of Satan I possess with might.
And, my ritual comes to close with sword held high.

# Unholy Enthronement

The burning of angels and their prophecy of shame,

It's Satan's minions of lust and fame.

Unholy enthronement we crown him our king,

No pain or suffering, our victory we sing.

Tormenting souls of the holy despised,

And raped then pillage the lambs of god,

I sent them destruction by my venomous rod.

My staff is in hand and my soldiers go marching,

Through the valley of holy and their brains are warping.

We conquer and defeat!

Unholy enthronement by the powers of hell,

The world I caught by satanic spell.

No more suffering of the satanic people.

(Sighs of relief)

Unholy enthronement,

No more of your sanctimonious cries,

No more of your prophetic lies,

And no more holy Christianized lives!

Unholy enthronement,

Its Satan's minions of lust and fame,

Unholy enthronement,

He's been crowned the king.

# Ritualistic Bliss

I have come almighty one!

You have called me?

Here I sat before your table to feast upon the swine,

And goat blood!

Where demons chant all around!

Hear the never ending motion of uproar!

Calling the seekers I command the joys of flesh.

Why must this be? Is it the infernally black?

It is so comforting in your presence.

Dark Lord Master Satan.

Speak to me!

You're the air I breathe!

Oh' how grateful for satanic plunder I am!

Oh' have I felt the real meaning of life while in your
arms warm embrace!

Dominus Inferus Vobiscum!

Salve!

Spiraling down into madness,

Little clown voices laughing sardonically,

And I hear them in my head.

The sound of rolling thunder,

And the vibration of a freight train at a high speed,

My heart pounds out of my chest.

Panic strikes with total fear!

Madness! Madness! Madness!

Screams fill the room.

I try to get a grip on things and all the sudden complete silence freezes over.

His voice speaks out:

"My son of Satan, I am Lucifer, Belial, Nergal, Baal-Berith, Dagon, Set, Amon, and all the nameless ones.

Therefore in you I am well pleased."

Laughs of celebration!

Shemhamforash!

Ask and it be granted!

He speaks again:

"You are favored by me child, great joys are coming your way, infernally yours."

It is done.

And so it shall be finished.

Hail to you child of night.

# CREATOR

From the time our journey began,

On earth as beast roaming free,

And holding sacred fire rites,

The moon was splendidly large.

Hecate the infernal teacher gave blessings to her children.

We were created by a cosmic explosion,

And radio-active particle that cooled on the earth's crust.

Life was born out of a nuclear synthetic waste,

And the formation of radiation to bond our form!

Atoms and molecules in their spasmic vibration,

The protoplasm the genetic make-up,

Of a newly formed alien called the human-animal.

Our creator is the very life that's in us,

And divinity of cosmic power!

The human-animal struggles for hidden truths outside themselves.

The answers lay within for the next cosmic working.

Energetic vibrating waves emanating from our own presence.

We are stars on earth.

SHINE!

"The means for serving the beast is accomplished by entering into compliance with your own heart. Therefore, serving your heart you have fulfilled the beast."

# Radiation

A created cosmic treasure,

Fulfilled energy existed by nucleo-synthesis.

Mutated and developed in a microwave.

Walking radiation, mutants all from the scattered stars,
as the seven were once joined as one.

The substances of four made us as one.

Through space time tragedies of those that light cannot
shine outward.

The spiraling down in retro-grade manner,

As we reach the final ending to a compact whole for
union once again.

Our stars are scattered and wings have become
shattered.

Creation in darkness,

Walking radiation as mutated stars,

We sink in the vortex of a black hole.

Infinite black vastness,

A variable finite ending in cosmic journey's,

We sink in the abyss.

Never-ending chills from the thoughts of outer-
darkness!

Our imagination's created a new thermal dynamic of a
coming nuclear holocaust.

Are we angels and demons destined to die?

By the same radiation that created us!

What's in the next coming if this one ends?

A newness of hydrogen and helium ignited by a spark!

A new creation of life!

Walking radiation as mutated stars,

We sink in a vortex of a black hole.

We have not the inclination to the heart of the matter,

The question has yet to be answered before the big bang.

Longing to understand the mysteries of creation and our searching never stops.

The fields of Mars and Venus created emotions of beautiful madness in love.

Our feelings are terrestrial controlled by celestial bodies of molecular matter.

Divided masses of spoken word,

Sound waves and thought patterns of a cosmic working.

Thermal therapy, the rise of temperature in a vibrating field of radiation!

We are the message sent by the universe!

The walking dynamics of thermal-radiance shinning in a complete darkness!

# Nuclear Fission

A fifty thousand degree burning nuclear fission takes place.

Born of creation out of the black vastness!

After billions of years the time had come,

For the creature of extra-terrestrial life!

Radio-active mutants, a whole planet of them!

Atoms forming and radiation procured,

From gases of space sent through time.

Life then exhales and oxygen spilled forth.

A creature walks!

Walking zombies with intelligence,

Just the radiation present!

How else could we explain existing life in a cosmic journey?

Nuclear fission at its best!

Nuclear fission put to test!

We've built bombs from the same concepts,

The invention for ending creation,

As the very thing that created us!

The power of many spheres and oracles were sought.

Brought on by nuclear fission,

This is mans vision!

(Pause)

Photons emitting dimly from the black stars,

Gravity allows it no escape!

Nucleo-synthesized by extreme heat causing a radio-
active glow!

Time has passed and the cooling begins.

Several gases create a shield and formed our elements.

Microwaves of radiation in the great black universe sized
up in theories of small minds.

Relaying messages, for a new nuclear fission!

Our ending is in the mind through future cosmic
theories.

I conquered destruction through the path of corruption.

I brought life through seduction.

The courtesy of satanic production!

Photo-synthesis reduction,

The black hole induction!

Infernal black visions of fire and ice division!

Satan's word incision!

A precision of the lower world far below!

Master, I am with you!

Infernal legions slash askew!

I conquered destruction through the path of corruption.

I brought life through seduction.

The courtesy of satanic production!

I stopped the self torture,

For Lucifer's light!

*Rev. Joshua M. Escritt*

I let the devil shine his brilliance in the black starry sky.

The four corners of earth according to Satan,

I champion with pride.

# Rite of Passage

For all those nights I spent with you,

Just to make me feel so blue.

Filled with love to be betrayed in blood!

Courtesy of falsehood!

As time past by, my life brought change,

Of satanic thought in acid rain.

I rose from emotional hindrance,

And my heart now mended with acceptance.

# Conquered Destruction

Started out with everything,

I had all to lose.

Driven by a drug,

Bloodied streets that show no love!

Still everything to loose!

Never looked back after rolling the dice,

The battling complexities of amphetamine Christ!

Virtual reality of a drugged paradise!

Embracing pain of the craving vein,

I stopped the self torture for Lucifer's light.

I let the devil shine his brilliance in the black night sky.

I've championed the devil with pride.

# The Question

When things start to fail and life is at its end,

What do we do, what do we say?

What's left?

And, who truly knows what is beyond this grave!

Verily, can we say is there life after death?

Or, will we shout with uproar to the sky with weeping
of sorrow?

Can things really be?

Or, is it just an illusion?

Why are things spoken into existence?

Or, could I be mad?

What is the meaning of all this?

Can we all get along without all this conformity?

Do you know what magnetism is?

When it comes to human existence!

Why do we have to become insane to find hidden truths
and complete truths?

Just to be considered sane!

Will the supreme-being ever stay strong?

What's the point of love when it comes to enemies?

Why the hate when it comes to dealing with loved-
ones?

Can there be true harmony?

Will there ever be real crystal clarity?

Is every-thing truly a selfish act?

Can these be the questions or put to the question?

The question!

# Changes

Changes!

It takes time to get things right.

Going through changes!

I never want to relive the past.

Life has caused some changes.

Apart I could have never learned.

Been sent through changes!

The struggles of everyday life caused some changes.

I never want to be alone through all my changes.

Emptiness and darkness within,

I made some changes.

Was filled with Enochian light,

My rituals for changes!

Only anger and no self control,

And I made great changes.

I don't know what to do or what else to say,

I live in a world where there is only selfish take.

The brutal selfish people,

When will I awake?

From this horrible nightmare,

A dream I cannot shake.

Changes!

Forced myself through changes!

If I had another day,

I'd surely spend with you,

I'd tell you I love you and miss you greatly too.

Forced me through those changes!

Finally I've made it.

# Thorazine Eyes

Thorazine eyes!

The pleasure beauty disguise!

Forfeit the savage mind,

The beast of torment sublime!

A wonderful bliss of a zombie kiss,

Given by the psychiatric risk!

For a chance at sanity,

Through Thorazine eyes!

Thorazine eyes!

For the future of promise,

In a drugged paradise!

Anything! Everything! A scream from a room,

To avoid the stray jacket and padded gloom!

I felt so bound by those leather straps,

Those five point restraints only made me laugh.

Through Thorazine eyes!

Catered by doctor's and a syringed high,

To stop the voices and my paranoid cry!

To find the peace and comfort inside,

I had to ride on the Thorazine high.

To slow my thoughts and hidden ghost,

To stop the screams of the nightmare host!

In the depths of Thorazine eyes!

Tattered and rugged,

The minds decay,

To balance my thoughts,

To feel hope of a better day!

Looking through Thorazine eyes!

# When

When the ancient city was sinking!

When we were losing our blood-lines history that was once original and tangible!

The ones who carried on the magical tradition of wisdom and everlasting glory!

When my people were seeking the light of truth!

But, then most became lost!

When our people stand strong in times of trials and tribulations!

When the beautiful love for one another and working in harmony searching out destiny!

When our ancestors are championed for our own inner strength!

Where beauty lays hold of our future children!

When the purity of our race finds their way back to the roots of our blood-line!

When drugs and the corrupt mind are laid to rest, so our future people can grow in wonder and delight, and do honor to the gods' up high!

Oh' how the stars move and the moon reflects its radiance onto their children of Odin!

Oh' how the battle hammer of Thor smashes the stillness of night and its sound of thunder!

By the gracious pale moon light, we children can see our way through the darkness!

And the peace shall be to the Norse Gods'!

# Drugged

I've lived out this burdensome life,

With contempt and strife!

It's always do or die,

In the fast lane trying to stay high!

The question is why?

I been there and done that!

Disappointed family and kids,

And I'm ruining my life for this!

Put into prison and loss of my freedom!

If you could sit him down,

You couldn't teach him.

Life has been a wreck on cocaine and meth!

Changed my addiction to alcohol and pot,

Only long enough to collect my thoughts.

Drugged, drugged I said!

Anything to kill this pain stuffing it down!

Fell off in a sea of alcohol this time for sure!

I'll soon drown!

A life full of drugs,

Exchanged it for a life full of love!

# Despicable Love Chapter

Alibis and questioning,

Testimonies of suffering!

Why the wasted love and energy?

For those that don't deserve it!

Why the mystical dream and paralization of another world?

The enemy shall surely kill you!

And the word kills personal freedoms.

All you have to do is read them.

Spiritual pipe dream!

Killed off a team of reality dream!

Winners choose wisely!

The Satanist mentality,

Christian love, just another brutality!

Seek personal freedoms,

And inside your satanic heart,

You shall find real love.

Despicable love chapter disintegrated!

# White Men

In domination we ride, this dark night that lives inside us to conquer all things.

Gods I say, I speak thy name. It's victory or die!

We stand as brothers of Satan. We have thrown out the mildew mind and brought forth genius.

So we have thrown out this land hungry for blood, the blood that is spilt into the devils cup. All I can see are the gods in the sky, the moon, and the stars.

Open to us for our fortune is due!

Hail the Lord master Satan!

Teach us wretched father the mysteries of your creation. Let us do honor for hell shall rise up!

In the blackness the screams I hear!

Their so close to me I feel them suffer!

The days turn to night and the sun shall fall,

Incinerate the Christian soul!

Death to all I blow the kiss, I have sealed your fate for eternity.

I glorify myself in this inhumane world,

And seek out the strong and I shall come!

Hail Satan.

# Satanic War

Avenge the kill.

The murderous thrill!

Politics of vengeance,

The blessings from hell!

Conquering the Christians,

They scream and yell!

Politics in blood,

This country has failed,

Brutal bodies burning,

A horrid putrid smell!

By the majesty of Satan,

Our victory our kill!

Running through the minions,

And burning heavens shell!

All of those who are burning have fallen from Jesus of Christ that has failed, to hold their ground in battle with swords.

Bloody pucking terror,

I'm burning the blackened corpse hair!

I'm the martyr for Satan,

I have no cares!

For all those vile Christians,

They waste our space and air!

Satanic war! Satanic victory! Satanic war!

# Longing For Home

Now at once I seek the beast!

Running towards the pentagram!

Dense darkness but a glow of embers!

A burning desire with a lustful member!

Seeking wisdom of arcane obscenities!

Forbidden fruits in close proximity!

Enforcing laws of satanic extremities!

Deification of corrupted life!

To find a whore to make her my wife!

I look to the deep-south and what do I see?

Fiery pits and circling demons,

Cheerfully! Shouts of joy!

All this time alone, my agony is gone!

Finally I found my real friends!

They've been in hell attending the party and feast.

I should have known this as my home!

Hell is my home and a refuge! A shelter from hypocrisy!

The fools who believed god to take them to the sky,

They vanished to hell to be tortured by hells children.

The Satanic truth and Christian lies,

The beating down of emotional brain-washing!

They blame us! US!

They murdered their own god and now seek to murder us.

For the crime of individuality and creativity!

The strong WILL survive!

And hell my home!

# Dark Desert Journey

Disciples of the heinous!

The virtues of darkness he gave us.

How long for our journey until we see Damascus?

Upon the sand dunes I saw his shadow.

Follow me under cumbersome stars and the moon will
be your light.

Everywhere I go I understand and I see.

A union, a bond with the dark one,

Caught up in emotional ecstasy!

In the dark desert I journey!

In the dark desert for eternity!

The horrid smell's of rotting flesh,

And eating of the tainted breast!

My madness to maintain survival!

Shunned and exiled to a place where I've been blessed.

For the price of betrayal and a royal courts lust!

I am a beast no longer man!

I wander the desert of burning sands.

In the dark desert I journey.

In the dark desert for eternity!

Oh' poisonous stars align yourselves right.

Let the powerful gods rise up.

From the deep on the ocean floor!

Atlantis will ascend forever more!

Ancient tongue and ancient mind,

Cast me in your likeness by an ancient rhyme.

Ancient dreamers awaken to me.

# Storming Hell

My infernal companions riding on the clouds!

As my chanting increases they cast down blessings to me.

Double lightning bolts of electric fire,

They are paralleling through the air.

I loll unto my dark lord father Satan.

He smiled down in grim darkness,

With thundering obscenities!

My protecting guidance and earthly success was granted.

The loud crack in mid air,

I penetrate the veil between worlds.

The blazing red glow on the east horizon,

I plunged down into the earth's cavern where I stay until the vanishing of the sun.

By the moon and stars I'm shone my sign.

Destined to dine in a dead body shrine!

Storming hell I seek my plunder,

Storming hell with sardonic thunder!

Violence and murder of Jesus, my wonder!

The thunders of black sky,

Raging with deadly sin and a murderous plight!

We fought in war by satanic light,

Deserted minions of Christian lies!

We stand on mounds of dead Christian foes!

Blood on our battlements,

And our exaltation or prolific goat!

Storming hell I seek my plunder,

Storming hell with sardonic thunder!

Storming hell in infernal wonder!

Hail Satan.

# CDartyr's For Satan

I'm proud to be Satanic, this I know I am free to be a god.

I will not forget those hypocrites,

Who caused me so much grief!

We stand tall and proclaim individuality!

For all my brothers of the left hand path, strength and bravery!

Murdering Christians in exalting the goat!

Come close to me so I can slit your throat.

Vengeance and purgatory is directed by me,

There is no punishment for the sinner, they are free.

Our vengeance my brothers by the satanic decree!

Martyrs for Satan! Martyrs for Satan!

We are proud to be fucking Satanist,

Where the power rises from Hell!

We will not forget those Christian bastards,

Who caused much herd conformity!

We stand tall and proudly proclaim,

Enforced brutality!

To my brothers of the left hand path,

Be thy fierce creativity!

Satanic martyrs!

# Abused Planet

Searching the cosmic answers,

For the existence of this life!

The microwave caused this life,

To multiply this earth!

Shielded by the ozone layer,

There's not much time left.

Sailing our journeys through the radiation,

Sea of darkness, looking for friends we never knew.

Blessed by thy knowledge and understanding!

But why,

Christianity would ruin it too.

Sailing on a magnetic field and tectonic plates cause her shake.

She is deeply scarred by the poisonous abuse.

She keeps patience and one day she will kill.

Mother earth floating on a whim in outer darkness!

The journeys path and finding treasure,

A place within for a new found pleasure.

Our guiding moon floating,

And infinite seas of gases!

What's in the next big creation?

Will we find our place in it?

The measure of one life is not enough!

To indulge myself in much!

The wonderers seek our praise.

Can we give them what they want?

The war has already started!

Let it finish to completion!

Along our path through outer-darkness!

# The Christian Murderers

The pucking pains and bloodied stains,

Of virgin prey and emptied veins!

Murder the holy of a vile Christ,

Unto the beast a paradise!

The repetitive incompetence of their glory divine,

Burning their heaven is not a crime.

A service for the beauty and free,

Exalted pagan prosperity!

A divine intervention is their chemical imbalance,

Of a fruitful narcotic that leads them to death.

Their consistencies of hypocrisy has killed innocent
blood,

A brutal homicide that the government led!

Christian brutality for conformity that have been
brought on with no laws to govern them!

These are the Christians who get away with murder.
That's not going to happen again.

We will show the psychological warfare!

Infernal dominion to the beast glorified!

Putred hatred vile poison burning in our heart for
revenge, to kill every Christian and maintain our grin!

# Two Dragons

Swirling thoughts of beauty and madness,

The curses and blessings done in vanity!

The seals of the dragon,

Dragon of water, dragon Leviathan!

Grew to a beast that holds water back,

For the human-animal not to drown!

She lies deep down in every man's heart,

A vision of beauty and nothing more!

The turbulent water remolds the shape,

Of earth and man, she will not desert!

Her charming companion helps her at work,

Behemoth of power, of blood, and of curse!

Every day we don't drown,

Is blessing in disguise!

Behemoth and Leviathan shall forever maintain!

The water so powerful gives creativity in pride,

For those who seek the satanic freedom.

With personal liberties, championed on high,

No brutal toxic Christian could stand alive.

Direct all your thanks for all those blessings!

The two dragons: Behemoth and Leviathan.

The two dragon's infernal reign!

1. It's all fun and games, until you burn a satanic witch on a stake. Then it's war!

2. All gifts come from Satan and curses from god. The weak and lowly will die from incompetence; the satanic people will endure forever.

# Hypocrisy

Hypocrisy burned in the devils name,

Hatred and prophecy show me thy flame!

Eternally black infernally exalted.

Halted Christianity they have spilt forth travesty.

Unto thy throne of Satan we bow!

Before thy majesty of victory we want.

Given thy power to conquer our foes,

Counter-productivity is their goals!

For their betterment of sheer hypocrisy,

They pray to their god.

To forgive them their sins so they can bloody their hands.

Fools and cowards I will burn too,

My victory by Satan!

I live forever more in the world of power,

And nine miles ahead of you!

On your corrupted smile,

Your incompetent guiles and hidden wiles!

Hypocrisy, you're fucking hypocrites! Hypocrisy!

# Brutal Beatings Battered Christians

Brutal beatings battered Christians!

A pile of flesh In Satan's minions!

Vile poison of your holy lies,

You brought it on by your guilt enterprise.

Bastards! I ravage through your army!

I strangle your Christ and his poisonous blood.

I killed off your lie of putrid hypocrisy that caused thy vile pains.

It's our vengeance!

Bastards and now your shame!

Brutal beatings battered Christians!

A pile of flesh in Satan's minions,

Fuel the fires with the holy vile and the weak,

To keep hell alive in torment the deep.

Sacrificed a bloody mess of Christians of Christian blood!

The warlike devils battle the end.

Brutal beatings battered Christians!

A pile of flesh in Satan's minions!

The vision of darkness and the things to come,

The slayers of holy light, the kingdom of Satan!

We stand and we fight!

Infernal demons!
Brutal beatings battered Christians!
A pile of flesh in Satan's minions!

# Intro Demons

I upon the blazing flames of justice to scorch Christians
and their Christ!

Brutal torture black decay,

A vengeful lust and the deceased day!

The light dispersed by thy darkness gloom,

For victory and power of Satan most high!

Honor in refuge by one man's speech,

The creativity parading through virtual realities of a
conquest preacher!

Teach me darkly the commanding host of a brutal
mentality of the horror ghost.

And the beast shall rise again!

Reign for ever brothers of night by lustful sins of
individuality plight.

Honored brothers from long ago we murder thy
Christians with alter ego.

Blessed truly are the sick for their clarity of seeing what
the blind man cannot.

For the future infernal bliss of satanic delights!

Hail Satan!

# Òemons 2

Upon the blazing conquest of demons marching forward in battle against Christ the holiest lie.

Infernal radiance of black thought forms by blessings of the infernal storm.

With thundering sounds of the beating drums and our victory we won against their heaven.

Ripping and tearing the holiest angelical flesh of spiritual hypocrisy they have abandoned their Jesus shrines.

The murderous smile and stalking stare, of satanic

Soldiers and burning their hair!

In thy candle thy flame prepared the lasting curse on heaven.

Infernal Demons!

# Murder For Vengeance

Murder for vengeance and sacrifice for contingence!

Brutality for their gift,

Blinded by the white light script!

Nevermore incompetent love of a dying religion that shown above!

The militia horses of hypocritical lust,

For the war we rush.

To end conformity that once silenced us!

Murder for vengeance the blood that we spill!

Murder for vengeance the cancers we kill!

To stop the way of white washed burdens!

We find our place with the stars,

For the radiant leaders of created independent prosperity!

10,000 screaming voices with outstretched arms in my dark places, and I lead them all to the burning fires.

The pits of infernal comfort,

And the lies of god are no more.

Murder for vengeance the cancers we kill,

To stop the ways of the white washed burdens.

Murder for vengeance, the blood that's been spilled!

Covered in sins those that we keep,

We've darkened our vestments by soaking them deep.

Cleansing the night of unwanted light,

Our visions to create for the blessings on Satan's night!

Murder for vengeance the blood that has been spilt and covered in sins of those that we keep.

Murder for vengeance the cancers we kill and we have stopped the ways of white washed burdens.

Murder for vengeance! Murder for vengeance!

(Pause)

Part 2

The desecration of another life,

For the reasons of not staying in line!

Never acceptance of a god holy faith!

To stratify and to glorify Satan's lullaby!

Marching stars a vision of ours,

The sky torn open at the coming of Mars the closest gift
from Venus, our satanic infernal gladness, the misery is
yours.

We indulge in the true gift,

This world and this flesh and our only chance for
fulfillment of plight!

Our journey through the destiny and ending fate,

We correlate by star formation a vision not late!

Synchronize with darkness so the flames burn bright,

Calculation atmosphere as one to the cosmic vibration
of the pulse of the beast!

In man just another instinct to verification to existence!

Our goals for success in the future deicide a time in life
to remove all the shit!

The beautiful upbringing of satanic adolescence,

And not corrupted by mainstream politics.

One by one deleting the weak,

For the prize of nobility and for our bloodline the kings
palace and our royal court!

I am the only judge who holds all judgment against my own self.

That I redeem myself something no one has the power to do.

I have risen above, and I oversee these activities of what man does to man.

I stand outside the line that holds to the government so-called norms.

Blasting this universe with independent thirst, standing in power, and strong in the night!

Welcome to the satanic throne of Amfire lore.

# Fucking Christians

The ghostly murders of our past,

With their burning poisons and hatred wrath!

Brought on by fear of their holy path!

Our ancestors deserved not your torture that was given.

Fucking Christians, I will murder you.

Fucking Christians I will torture you.

You killed those people in brutal cold blood.

Your incompetent gospel of love, all I see is murder and hate.

You fucking hypocrites I surely can't wait.

Fucking Christians I will torture you.

Fucking Christians I will murder you.

In my empire your foul vapor of stale heaven and burning angels.

You incompetent hypocrites of your hatred in love!

You sang your songs while we remained in silence,

Now we shout back with individual pride.

You've wasted our time and now we give you torment sublime.

Fucking Christians I will murder you.

Fucking Christians I will torture you.

Fucking Christians we want payment in blood.

# Infernum Majestatis

Come, satanic storm hailing iniquities and slashing the light from Satan's throne.

Darkness en-shrouds me to fulfill the destiny of an apocalyptic war!

Gods of darkness chanting the sounds of night to bring forth delight.

Legions of demons parading the earth where hypocritical lives stay!

They hide in terror at the victory of our satanic flesh.

We purge the earth with lustful delights to watch them run in a curious flight.

The devils best in the darkness plight!

Veiled by honor and self preservation to stare into infernal creation of the new individuality!

Bringing forth a wretched disaster upon Christians with the purest originality!

The stench of Christian bull-shit of their guilt-ridding corruption, of white-light plagues!

Onslaught! The Satanic rise!

Power and glory and victory!

In Satan's name!

Infernum majestatis!

Infernum we claim with power and fame.

The powerful flame of darkness that provides our strength!

Infernum majestatis, corpse burning Christian!

# Blasphemy

Blasphemy of your son a begotten host of heaven!

Brought your blood to fruition of rotting incompetence
of a disastrous love!

The despicable creation of softness of a law so
incompetent in the lasting preservation!

Conquered thy kingdom you bastard son!

Blasphemy of the dark psyche!

Blaspheme the holy-spirit!

Blaspheme all night!

The coffin opens for the Nosferatu to roam this
blasphemed earth.

To drain the blood of the incompetent mirth!

Upon these winds ye shall know,

The bloodied plagues of Christianities end.

We proclaim rule of a satanic earth.

Blasphemy of the dark psyche!

Blasphemy to the holy-spirit!

Blaspheme all night!

The doors unlocked to the tales of creation,

The blood and all this desolation too!

Desecration of the next brutal massacre!

A holy mans nightmare!

Blasphemy of the dark psyche!

Blaspheme the holy-spirit!
Blaspheme all night!
We sing and they scream!
Blasphemy! Blasphemy!

# Responsibility

A man has no business telling of another's business.

If a man render's consequence because of a failed situation, he then has no right shifting blame upon another for his consequence. Ultimately he chose his situation and it is he who is responsible for his circumstance.

If a person gets in the business of chance and is after his gain, but is unwilling to accept the possibility of loss or defeat on his own part from any situation, then the individual has no business getting involved.

A man of honor and respect will lay down his life for his fellow friends and or his brotherhood, if it is called for. This keeps solid structure and strength.

Responsibility is a tall order that the many cannot maintain. Only few can and are holding strong their duty and responsibility to the life they live.

Poser's who are wolves in sheep's clothing are continually trying to infiltrate our very circles of superiority. Those poser's are a plague that if they were allowed would send us to ruins.

These weak individuals and their insecurities will surely make them vile. Their vileness will cause famine in the worse ways.

Our faculties cannot allow our intelligent eyes to become lazy. Our structure calls for the constant weeding out of the very weak.

I say to you that only the strong will survive and endure. Responsibility will also mean and follow; silence and secrecy. Silence and secrecy becomes broken when an outsider learns of vital information that happens within any respected circle.

Society has far too long, ran around with knowledge that don't belong to them, that should have never made it outside of the honored circle. This results in an irresponsible individual and disloyal behavior. The irresponsible individual who said one to many words has in actuality created an existing plague. If the plague lands on deaf ears of the weak, will more than likely cause the collapse of organized group activity. This irresponsible individual will be the responsible party for this destruction.

When we become part of something or anything for this matter, we are given some sort of responsibility and we have to be willing to fully carry out that duty. Remember these keys for success:

- Responsibility
- Silence
- Secrecy
- Honor
- Loyalty
- Respect

You noticed I never listed trust. This is because 'Trust' can lead to blindness. Blindness to destruction! I say always harbor doubt in everyone and everything. Harboring doubt will keep you on your toes, so when someone or something causes a problem or collapse in our organized groups and elsewhere for the matter, your let down and the shock won't be as detrimental to you. Also, to fix the situation in any method necessary to keeping the structure in tact without the detriment! As you will have calculated every situation and individual as possible cancers!

Responsibility is a word that carries heavy weight of vital importance. So, I ask you this question: Why, the large masses of people customized themselves to think and believe that 'responsibility' should be taking lightly?

My answer to this question will be only part of the whole answer and each person will carry a piece of the whole answer to make the answer whole and unified.

People have no desire to be held responsible for their actions. These people fear loss of freedoms and they fear death, and anything else that fear overwhelms them with. Christianity plays a large role in brainwashing large masses into shunning responsibility for their actions and choice. They teach that consequence is caused by someone else and or the devil. These people make for a disposable society. We have to annihilate all of them or they will annihilate us!

# A Person's True Worth

A person's true worth depends on what his capabilities are. Morals and values will make up a person's actions!

A real convict shows no mercy or weakness when it comes to winning at all costs. For example: I know of a person who has very little or no concern for the public or law-enforcement. The individuals not going to allow anything or anyone to stand in their way, even at the cost of all freedoms and or loosing their own life! The only thing that matters is he accomplishes what he set out to do. The individual will believe this to be normal and acceptable behavior. In return he shows no remorse for his actions. After the individual has rendered severe consequence for his actions, only finds himself plotting his next ruthless scheme of the century. Enough is never enough. Consequence has no meaning or value to the individual. There's no rock bottom. Only life and death, situation and circumstance, black and white! No excuses, things happen because they happen, it's meant to be. There is no divine intervention other than the human-animals very divine intellect. His brain and body is responsible for all his own worldly affairs. His success and failures, blessings and curses!

To succeed in his endeavors with no cares or conscience he holds on to anger, rage, resentments, sorrow, and never stops his mourning of his cherished companions. He would say: 'My pains are the great motivator for ensured success and pleasures.'

He will spend much time and effort in reeling in his victims, making them think that he is a trusted servant, only to strike them down like the human animal prey they are. He only makes and holds dear a small handful of close friends he remains loyal to and honors. As he despises the whims of the many and uses the many in the "Infinite Game of Puppeteering" and they are the game pieces he uses in the practice of manipulation and deception. He does this by creating an illusionary big picture that everyone is focused on, while the real big picture takes place off the scene.

These victims have been stripped of their pride without them even knowing it. The programming of the individual and the mass herds has become easy. He has come to understand the human animal's behaviors and the cycles of every age. He firmly believes in himself with all confidence. He boldly states: 'I am the highest of all living creatures, all demons and devils, all gods of the past-present-and future. Bow down before me at my command for I am the Just and loyal companion to all infernal affairs, and delights of the flesh. These things are owed to me!

So say's my understanding.'

# The Misconceived Satan

There are a lot of young audiences out there getting brainwashed by television and Christian families. These people mistake Hollywood movies for reality. It's only fantasy, so they don't understand. These people are a mainstream conformity and are easily brainwashed to the illusions. They've accepted these things as facts. People who consistently do things that cause their destruction over and over again are not satanic. They are only guilty of stupidity and ignorance. The necessity to questioning everything leads people to wisdom and sound mind. The corrosion to the mainstream conformity is very thick and leaves much work to be done within the real satanic groups.

Our job is to keep advancing to higher roles and protect our own brotherhood from Christian poisons that have impacted us in a horrible way.

The devil and the devils children are the real owners of all that money those hypocritical Jesus preachers bilked from other Jesus slaves that had paid the rent and bill of the preacher.

The fake satanic groups have given their worship to Hollywood and Christianity by falling into their delusion. Under no circumstance or condition does a real Satanist give up superiority to be slave.

Satanic life is about indulgence and material gain and lust for life. There is no gain in death only loss.

Enjoy life with heart content!

# Master and Pet

When an owner gets a pet the pet becomes real close to the owner. When the owner beats the pet repeatedly what happens? The pet will shy away and hides because the pet no longer trust the owner. The same principal with family and friends too! When dishonesty and disloyalty, betrayal and violence happens' to another family member or friend, which shows a history, then, the same occurrence takes place.

"We cannot afford to be so shallow minded"

# The Big Scheme

I found through past experience that when a company or individual comes out with a new product, they say it is 100% guarantee, as you should already know that is bullshit. These drugs may work for some but not for others. That's what they should guarantee. All these companies talk shit about one or the other.

These companies guarantee themselves while degrading other companies while making themselves feels better. They need to take a look at their own product. They are only out for one thing and that would be your money. They can care less rather or not the drug even works. You see everyone is different and it's going to take something different for each and every individual.

# Siblings

When two people have children, the children tend to follow certain patterns. While it be two brothers or two sisters or brother and sister, it don't matter. When they are born close to the same age they grow up fighting with each other over stuff such as: toys and attention. If one has the lead by 4 or 5 years of age over the other sibling the situation would then alter as such: the older one has grown out of that stage of importance, while the younger sibling is just entering that stage of importance in their life. The love for each is potentially stronger and healthier with the expanded age difference. With the age difference being right around the corner, would cause many issues un-necessary to a healthy relationship. Note: siblings will love each other no matter what and their age difference makes all the difference in the world rather than the struggle of getting along is there or not.

People take life for granted until it is too late and until they have been awakens, and their eyes opened through situations of all sorts. Realize the now older ones, the impact of your actions that you have on your younger siblings! You may not see it openly. It may be kept to themselves because they love their older brother or sister and they don't know how to approach them.

# Keeping Perpetual Motion

There's nothing after death so our indulgence of what the world has to offer is only to live this life the best we can. The ones who abstain from the worldly pleasures end up having miserable lives on mythical whims of spiritual pipe dreams.

A Satanist is constantly gaining knowledge and understanding to the ways of the world. We don't take anything for granted. It is necessary to leave room for doubt and questioning. We are very responsible for all our own actions and I feel that responsibility is a must when you have important knowledge and understanding.

My final note is: working in accordance with self-knowledge.

# Dawn of Time

The consistency of water in a pregnant woman is the same consistency as the ocean water! I have a theory, maybe true or false, but I give no credit to this supposedly holy entity god. I say nature has its way of doing things. The lightening is made up of 100% protoplasm. The human-animal was and is constructed of mostly protoplasm and the other part water. Scientifically proven! The result of this is called "duality of nature" it takes male and female to create life. Unholy fuck! That kills the one god theory that is only masculine, oh' shit; I think I am on to something Satan! Can I get a hellish applause genius? That god and the Christians call father along with their heaven, easy to explain: Father Sky and mother earth. So, that god is guilty of sleeping with a whore! I wonder how much she costs! Infernally with barbarous delights!

# Candle

The candle has the ability to change many forms. Its life is frozen in time, waiting for the person to come to give it the candles soul-mate. At last the candles brought to life with a single flame. The warm embrace of a magical moment! Its time is short and serves the greatest purpose though. Its life is the most meaningful. The flame is the heart of the candle. Our desires manifest within the flame.

The candle another form of communication within our own selves! It tells us many things by the way the flame dances. The questions are is it bright or dim? Is it tall or short? What is its color and can it be blue?

The candle is romance, the candle is love and it is hate, used at night and used at day. It sparks an interest in the mind. I am old and I am new. I have been here since the beginning of time. Watch and you can hear my message. I want to give you a piece of my light and light is love.

# Who is Who

Having the ability to see things for how and what they really are. Not easily misled into brainwashed beliefs. Not believing everything you hear about religion and some other things. Don't take things for granted. Investigating things already investigated. Questioning everything! Knowledge is power and it being and having independence from all and committed to self. Not giving up to unseen gods or goddess' by worshipping that entity. Instead, worshipping yourself as a god amongst men in the flesh. Believe in yourself! Just be yourself! We are the truth of all things by seeing through the hyped up propaganda of a fake world. Look people, this is about knowing yourself and being unique in every way. Looking to gain complete understanding of the mind and awareness of the outside influences! Needing to understand this system of things and totality! Being a leader! Having a unique outlook on life and being able to give a Satanic perspective on various situations. The ability to pick out things like music, movies, clothes, groups of people, and even individuals that are not following the herd. Also, seeing all the things that are programmed by the world ect. ect. ect.

Majority of the world have been blinded to the truth of things and they have taken things way out of context. These such, people have been fooled by the new aged god call HIM: Television! While Christianity is in turmoil and chaos, fighting over their spiritual pipe dreams, we Satanist are about our vital existence. We love and enjoy life and this will be our final result! Others end up hating themselves and or committing suicide. Too bad for them! Ha! Ha! Oh' how I laugh at their hypocritical self deceit.

We could call this world a circus at the zoo. I value the life of animals over a lot of humans.

# The Christian Fear and False testimony against the Satanist

The Christian fear was brought on by the very human who created their beliefs. Their fear is their own Jew hell of torture for eternity and I tell you there is no such place.

The false testimony against the Satanist is what has kept their churches full of money. They go to church to preach and teach blame of the devil for all misfortune in life.

Satanist, have been slandered for many years by the Christian jerks. The truth of the matter is the Devil-Satan did not make you do anything. Satanists are responsible for our own actions and behaviors. My final words to Christian creeps: "You made your bed now lay in it".

# Christian hate towards the Satanist

Hatred has been the number one focal point by the Christians and their communities all over the world. They have not focused at all on their own progress, following their own philosophy, and teachings.

Their holy writ states that they are to love everyone from good to bad! So, why are these Christians not following what is supposed to be their beliefs and their laws?

The Christians focus has always been to destroy all others, slander, preach lies for truth, and all other talks against the devil and the Satanist.

It is then true, Christians don't believe in their own sacred text.

Christianity will soon self-destruct and the devil will then get his due.

# hell

Hell is an atmosphere here on earth in this world of flesh. Hell is only one side of a individual. Its other side is heaven that is necessary for creating the balance within the human mind.

Many people choose to live out the hell side of themselves by their stupidity that causes their own pain and misery. An example of something that causes their own, pain and misery; It Is a Crime, my definition of a crime is taking something that does not belong to you. The end result is Stupidity. This results in loss of freedom and causes misery.

People who beat women and children, including child molestation, and animal mutilation that is not satanic and is the principle of the misconceived Satan! The point I am trying to make is after death there is no place called hell where you are tortured. That was a scare tactic by Christians to get you to conform to their beliefs and stay in line.

# Jesus lies and what accuser?

For hundreds of years now, Jesus freaks, have been preaching their own mythologies as realities. Brainwashing people with empty words that they claim to be heavy lies upon the Satanist, those that they were directed against! Jesus lies have already gotten millions of our honored brothers and our Ancestors killed. It is time to put a stop to all Christian's madness.

The question is: What Accuser? I tell you the truth, the accuser is on earth and they are human-animals, they are called Christians. They are the ones who consistently blame and accuse the devil and the Satanist.

1.  From whence I came, there I shall go back to.

2.  My fortune and virtue lays hold in this life, so why must you make attempts to sway me on to your spiritual-pipe dream.

3.  I have conquered many things, and in my moments of solitude, my blood hath strengthened in my resolve.

# Christian Guilt

For the last 2000 years since their Jesus walked the earth, they have been preaching to feel bad for what you do and to suffer. Its teachings are based on the person to suffer in misery and pain.

It makes no sense to indulge your selves in self-destructive behavior. Why live out death? When you can live out life and indulge in the pleasures of the flesh, to rejoice and delight in the worldly embrace.

I tell you the truth, don't do things you're going to regret later, just be glad that you have done whatever it is you do.

Guilt is the number one killer and is the cause of mans fall many times. Have no regrets and need not repent for any of your own doing. Be happy and satisfied!

# Rebirth and Resurrection

There's no life beyond the grave and there's no torment either. Rebirth and resurrection only take place through the process of sexual intercourse by male and female called sexual conception.

In order for you to be reborn and resurrected you would have to die or a part of you would have to die, then would have to give of you in order to bring something new.

During sexual intercourse the male releases his DNA in to the female. His DNA is now divorced and no-no-longer alive in him. A form of death of himself! The female is where the death of the male goes like a graveyard to wait the process through rebirth of male DNA. The females DNA is given to the death of the male DNA to form rebirth. Once the human animal child becomes the resurrection of both its parents by genetic gene-pools!

This is the process called reasonable and logical thinking to explain reality for what it is, instead of telling a fantasy lie.

# Death

The ceasing of all functions of life! Sin is making an unclear judgment in life's situation. The end result is stupidity the number one satanic sin. We exalt life and we live it to the fullest and value the here and now. Indeed we hold dear and acknowledge our very deaths. Suicide is a weakness they have not found the meaning of life or any reason to live.

Death is the opposite of life meaning non-existence, having no feelings, emotions, movements and no senses. In death nothing exist no memory just dense darkness, completely black.

The spirit is just pent up energy that leaves the body when death occurs. That energy goes back into the atmosphere to be recycled also known as reincarnation or calling it a past life, but this has been mistaken.

# Blood

The most sacred and most powerful life force where the soul lives!

The wannabe Satanic groups have taken on the concepts of what (Hollywood) has made on their movies and what Christianity or Christians have labeled people who are not of god as. These things are: animal sacrifice, human grown or baby sacrifice, drinking of blood, and child abuse or neglect. These things are not part of Satanism at all. The drinking of blood will and can spread diseases. Self-Preservation is the highest law of nature.

# Music

It's the most powerful source to conjuring and very evocative to the human psyche. Music causing the neurotransmitters to fire rapidly creating over stimulated feelings within oneself. Within this process is a strong induction of memories coming to the surface causing emotional euphoria. Within this state of being, it opens pathways of thinking to help aid an individual in learning, meditation, and stronger emotional feelings of thinking and planning of the future, taking a look at the past, and seeing our present. The emotional response in the human psyche is essential to the production of motivation. Emotion will cause desire. Desire will bring fulfillment.

# Acceleration

The mind is very powerful and the greatest things have manifested through a person's thinking. Thinking causes action. Action sprouts behavior. A person's success and failure is a direct result of their own thinking. A person only acts according to the way of their own thinking. What your senses bring in, your behaviors spill out. A person's carelessness and no self control is what cause consistent failure and misfortune. These individual's priorities for success are not intact. The reorganization of thought process and new enlightenment will ensure the individual their personal success. To do this a very extensive self-analysis will be required based on personal necessity.

Understanding is the key to the mind. The ritualization of thoughts and feelings is freeing your self from imprisonment of self. Ritual is the best form of self counseling and you save lots of money in the long run by not going to some qualified assistance to tell you how to live your life. A person is sure to get results from the process of ritual. Rituals will come in many forms and some maybe for group involvement.

Ceremony is necessary for the reassurance of great accomplishments and life itself. Ceremony brings great joy to the heart of the individual celebrating because something wonderful has happened in a person's life. This is a time for splendor and greatness, a time for renewal.

Remember that study and understanding is the most important.

# Mind Altering Drugs

It has now become the 21rst. Century and still the many have been lured in to the world of drug. The population and their demand for these self destructive chemicals have grown increasingly strong. These individuals that have been hook line and sunk, one time had great potential instead they threw it all away to become a slave to the very drug they are using.

The methamphetamine epidemic is out of control and people are doing anything for another high. They would kill a friend and rob their own family, even sell their own children just to get the next fix. What a disposable society.

Mind altering drugs cause stupidity in the worse way and kills off the real person at hand. The euphoria and hallucinations fill you with false precepts and leads you to believe you can accomplish anything on them. In reality the drug just takes your mind off the real fact that you're dying with every dose of the drug. It kills the inner most part of a person's individuality and personality.

My people understand the ways of the world. There are better ways to dealing with your cares and concerns, pains and sufferings, revenges and blessings.

The Serpent hath spoken!

# Television: Hollywood and their Money

People are always in the mood for good entertainment. Society is very easily misled by the new god. Call it television and Hollywood is their personal Jesus. It all starts out in good fun until people start accepting fiction for fact.

Hollywood's not at fault but the audiences are! This is why: young audiences think that Hollywood entertainment is a promotion to commit heinous acts of violence in the way of a supposed satanic life. They call themselves Satanist. I tell you the truth these individuals who commit these heinous acts of violence are not real Satanist. These heinous acts of violence are as such: animal cruelty, animal and human ritual-sacrifice, drinking blood, child stealing, child abuse including child molestation, harming women and children in any way, and suicide. This is to name a few of the unimaginable things these people do. These are the individuals that are giving the real Satanist a bad name.

All these people who have condemned the Satanist based on television and their own personal hate, probably never picked up any real satanic literature to read. These people have no understanding. These people are God Damned, idiots. These individuals need to be annihilated to make this world a better place.

# Wars

For many years now there has been constant bloodshed over religious beliefs. For what reasons each group or religious sects are making attempts to bring herd conformity. These groups claim superiority in the excellence of their god.

The phrase: "who so ever shall lose his life, will gain eternal life and who so ever shall love his life, will lose it". Talking about this world! I believe this phrase has been taken way out of context and inverted to wreak havoc, man against man. If it were not for the lovers of life on earth, then perhaps this world could not continue to exist. The question is why are religious faith's based on the worship of a one god theory trying to force people to stay in line? Is their blind faith and their holy text the main driving force to their own delusion and insanity? Has the focus of these many different religious sects lost sight of their own personal progress and now focusing their energy on destroying all individuality and creativity? Yes, it has been said and it is very true: "we are all predatory animals by instinct, and it is self preservation that lays hidden until the proper moment calls when the human-animal's life is threatened. Self-preservation is what keeps the human-animal's life in continual motion. The combination for the continuance of the flesh is self-preservation in the lover of life in this world. So why, must these other religious sects demand rigorous hatred, pain, misery, suicide for the "GREATER GOOD", and murder?

The religious wars and murders that the Christian, Muslim, and Jews have brought on has been a lasting curse upon people's blood-lines for many generations.

This age and night has become psychological warfare by the many religious sects founded on a one god theory by their attempts at brain-washing anyone who is easily misled, including young children who cannot escape the holy-roller white-washed parental guidance, who hath left them no choice in the matter.

# Genealogy of Opposites

Christianity has brought chaos and disorder into this world. Their quest for world domination by means of murder and slander to my Ancestors who are the Satanic Nation! All the witch burnings are for what? The answer is this: Christians are such low life pathetic creeps and scum. Christians have shoved blame upon everyone else that's not of themselves and especially the **"DEVIL"**. Christianity is doing everything they can to put this world into slavery by making attempts to take away individuality from mankind.

Christianity is going to any lengths to brainwash children at an early age, by placing their holy writ concepts in the school systems where young children are unable to escape it. These Christian school teachers are deadly venom to our society and the advancement in evolution of the flesh. Christianity is making attempts to save the world by killing it, hell they can't even save themselves from themselves. Their life is death and our death is life in this world. Nothing after this world exists beyond our humanly flesh of life. Joy to the flesh!

In the eyes of Satan we are workers of creativity. We stand in individuality. Broke and breaking the cycle of herd-conformity. Christianity will preach freedom and peace while they practice slavery and murder. On the other hand us Satanists are the opposite of all other religions. We can care less what other groups are doing because we are not following them. Our life journey is to believe in ourselves, being superior as gods in the flesh, individuality, and creativity. We are masters not slaves.

The abstract thinking of Christianity is to not live

up to their own philosophy by going against their own holy writ. They leave behind their very foundation of love by indulging themselves in hate and murder against Satanists. Christianity is dying by their own curse. Christianity teaches you to suffer, to hope, to not have anything, give up your hard earned money in order to be saved, misery, depression, to not accept any responsibility for any of their own misfortunes, and failures. They teach to blame the devil for all wrong by them things. Christianity wants you to have remorse, but wait! For what! Have guilt! For what! Christians blame Satan, so why ask for forgiveness? Why feel bad for something if you're not at fault or blame? Well then, this theory makes me ask this question: shouldn't the devil be the one repenting and not human's?

On the other hand, us Satanist except responsibility for our own actions and for our own misfortunes! We know it is natural to make mistakes. It is no-longer a mistake when the same thing is repeated over and over again. It becomes intentional; then, there is no point in saying sorry or feeling bad for whatever the cause. **AVOID SLAVERY** and **SUFFERING**. If you're a Satanist, then you will have no regrets and your death is it natural, will end gracefully.

# Rules of Engagement

1. **Patience:** patience is a major requirement for things to go natural. Don't force anything. Things that are forced to happen when time or circumstance has not permitted it usually end up in failure and become a serious burden upon that individual. Why make an unnatural move that is going to more than likely bring lose and misfortune. So have patience.

2. **Intelligence:** be wise in every move you make, we cannot afford to make mistakes. Study will bring knowledge. History will bring future experience. Experience brings wisdom. A wise man thinks things through completely on both the positive side and the negative side, then, comes to a balanced solution.

3. **Honor:** your word is everything. If you give an oath, then keep it. If, you say it and mean it, then, find a way to maintain it. Honor is meant for brotherhood, family, friends, and intimate relationships. Live up to your own expectations. Don't set the standard so high where you fail. Start small. My final words on honor are: Strength-Loyalty-Unity.

4. **Don't show your anger in a heated moment:** giving control over you is the roots that grow deep and bring forth self-destruction. It is another form of enslavement unto that very thing or person. Anger in a heated moment sprouts "Stupidity" and stupidity brings disorder and your own fall.

End result, death or imprisonment. By remaining the gentlemen it will cancel out those who try to read your very action by each situation. In return, you become the mystery man that nobody can understand. People get more pissed off when they are unable to push your buttons, because you don't respond the way they want you to. There is always something in store.

5. **Play like a snake:** a snake slithers through the grass, cracks, and crevices unseen. The snake is doing the darker work that nobody has a clue about. He is left a mysterious stalker in the night. The snake comes into play, off to the side where the major things are happening. These are the things that main-stream don't see. This happens when they are focused on the illusion of what they think is the big picture. People are easily fooled. They would not know what to look for even if they were shown. If people could understand the real concepts of illusions, misdirection, deception, and manipulation then there would not be anymore entertainment for the world. The true forms of lesser and greater magic.

6. **Vengeance:** let no wrong go unpunished against yourself, family, and friends. Get rid of the problem in any manner necessary to make sure the justice has been served. "Trust not others of law to base your personal right." Take matters into your own hands, enough said.

7. **Investigate:** don't take things for granted and don't buy into rumors and gossip. Listen to the

information that is being brought to you. Take note of it if need be. Then go the heart of the matter and confront the situation at hand. If there are real issues at hand, then they need to be addressed in whatever manner necessary to achieve successful ends.

8. **Loyalty:** loyalty is a commitment that you make with a person, soul-mate, group, job, kids, friends, and all family. It is a bond between you and the other that outside influences cannot destroy. If you are loyal to something or someone, then you stay loyal to the grave. If loyalty is broken between the two, then the person's loyalty needs to be questioned from the very start. The loyalty that was broken was only in it to get what they want then get out by betraying the other. Loyalty is when you go to any lengths to stand up, defend, and help the other when times are hard or when the other is in need. Loyalty is not forsaking the very thing or person you are connected to.

9. **To live like a dove:** this, not saying, to be good guy. This belief is to help ensure success in worldly affairs. People don't pay others any mind who self-destruct and doom themselves to failure. Can a major drug lord or terrorist give good council to the world in public broadcast about saving people's lives and cleaning up the environment, while the world already knows who and what they are? Do you think they would listen? Living like a dove requires keeping his own house in order and conducting fair business, giving and receiving of fair value. Keeping the customer

satisfied by giving them what they pay for. To maintain proper family affairs. Give good council when council is needed and this will bring great success, respect, and honor.

10. **Never display any kind of weakness:** weakness that others see in you, they will use to their advantage against you. You then would be placed at their mercy as the inferior one who is being dominated. Never assume the role of slave. Ask yourself this question: what is the cost? Weakness leads to fear. Weakness will destroy you, although fear is an awesome motivator to bring forth self-preservation. Many people have conquered lots of things behind fear. People's beliefs and values will determine their weakness's, also, based on how they were brought up from childhood environment. If a person who has only had success in communicating and getting things done in an environment where he is surrounded by all women, then surely he has not learned to work with all men. The individual's weakness would be working and talking with all males. This is only an example, as there are many other weakness's that can lay dormant.

11. **Sacrifice:** sacrifice requires giving up something either permanently or even temporary in order to accomplish something much greater. This sacrifice maybe friends, family, places, or things that are going to slow down or even prevent the very goal you are trying to achieve. If, the very things and people you have sacrificed temporarily even loved ones, and they don't understand, then,

a healthy explanation with all respect to those you have set aside should understand. If, they truly care about your progress and success, or if, there is no understanding from the others, then, another choice needs to be made. This choice is: do you not sacrifice? And keep a few happy people and stay exactly where you are with no chance of accomplishing those certain goals for success, or let a few be angry and follow through with your original goal for the greater cause and in the end you gain much respect from the many? Might I say, the first choice would end up causing resentments and hate toward the very one's you refused to sacrificed temporarily because of their feelings of you leaving for awhile. Why should you suffer for other people's happiness? You need to choose what is best for you! You are never going to be able to make and keep everyone happy, satisfied, and content. So, start doing for yourself and everything else will come.

12. **Secrecy:** the power of silence is the key to freedom, understanding, and knowledge. When one's mouth is running, then he is not listening. Scare tactics of the government and all law enforcement ensures you with threats of imprisonment if you don't speak. I tell you not to do their work for them. They are looking for people to do their job for them to collect the pay check for a job well done by a piece of shit rat. There is no room for weakness in a house full of warriors. Weakness shall soon perish from the face of the earth. The merit and reward in maintaining secrecy no matter

what the cost is that of unity and solid structure. People need to be put to severe testing without them even knowing it, to see how true they really are or if they end up being a poser. Cops will lie in many circumstances to get you to sing like a fat girl performing an opera. These cops will play one against another just as for example: your partner said you committed the crime. While the other cop is telling the other partner he is talking against the one. Don't fall for that pathetic scheme the cops are trying to pull. Remain silent! If they are going to charge you, then, there will be proof of some sort. Ask yourself this question: is it worth running your mouth to take down a group? And for this your consequence shall be the loss of your life because your, too many words that needed not be. Your family shall or may end up suffering from it too. The second secrecy is intended for magical groups such as covens. We don't fear outsiders, it is just that they don't need to know our most sacred and personal things that sustain us in our private life. There are no needs to advertise these magical abilities to a large mass of people meaning society. Those people who talk up a good game are probably the least magical.

# Condensation

A person's fight for his own life depends on if they have anything worth fighting for. If a person finds no meaning in life, then it is easy for them to give up and not fight at all.

Many individuals in the world have not found the meaning of life. These people have been abandoned by friends and family. Other people have forgotten what life is really about!

These are my reasons: The government dollar has driven people mad. It has become survival of the fittest and who will win?

# Blowjobs by Jesus the Hypocrite

Jesus used both forms or I should say all forms of magic that he says you're condemned for. These would be: witchcraft, sorcery, alchemy, and necromancy. Jesus used conjurations and invocations. He also used levitation.

According to his word in the Old Testament a person would be condemned to hell for torment, if these things were practiced. This be the case Jesus is guilty of heresy and very ungodly things according to his hypocritical teachings. He must have gone to the very hell he created.

Even the holy writ says the demons and spiritual forces of darkness have taken over the heavenly realm. This is the New Testament writings. How much more do the satanic brothers have to prove?

Christianity has slandered Satanism for several years. They have learned murderous literature that's not part of Satanism. Christian's accuse us by that, their, own mystical belief.

Indeed, the one man who created the Christian belief, those who wrote their mythical stories was successful in gaining each individual person. There is one guarantee and that is everyone will die eventually.

Take for instance, the pharmaceutical companies as we speak. They charge hundreds of millions of dollars to people who have H.I.V. or even full blown Aids and other cancers for antibiotics and other medications. They are only designed to slow down the process of them dying. This prolongs their agony of knowing they are going to die anyway, despite their efforts of going financially bankrupt.

The drug companies thrive off of seeing people stay in misery and pain of knowing they are going to die, to have to give up their last dollar to stay alive one more day. The pharmaceutical companies know damn well they have a found a drug to get rid of the supposed incurable disease. They won't let loose of it because if everyone became well, the drug companies would go broke. These, such companies would rather rob you of everything you own and your family, to leave you dead!

# The Nine Stimulations

1. **Sloth:** is an action of reluctance, wanting to sleep in until afternoon or night by not wanting to get up, instead, just lying around in bed. There was this man who spent his whole life enjoying himself by only being motivated to do and get things done in and on his own time. He felt that the bed was the most peaceful and comfortable place to be, except maybe the bathroom. He would rather live as the Hermit because that's when he accomplished the most. He listened and understood his own thoughts as revelation, and he being the most inspired at these times. Anyway, my point is relaxed and does what is most natural to you when it comes to slothfulness.

2. **Envy:** wanting whatever other people have can only be a wonderful motivator to help aid your own self-will in getting and accomplishing things on your own terms. Envy is another method of inspiration and inspiration becomes accomplishment. How can you possibly want something that you have not seen personally? This person had a bestial craving of the worldly indulgence. Wanting a married man's wife for a night, peering into other people's lives, necessitating the carnal instinct, the pulsating rhythm through his body of demon's blood and wanting everything not of his.

3. **Gluttony:** the act of eating until your heart's content. In some aspects gluttony is strength.

It takes food to survive. A hard worker and or creative person to bring in the money to eat. Pride will help you lose weight if need to be. Why feel bad for eating until your heart is content. Enjoy! Delight! Indulge! Feast!

4. **Greed:** why hast thou accused me? For I only want for me the many worldly things and I don't want to share these things, therefore the many are not, deserving. Greed the action of wanting more than your fair share. Who is to decide how much is enough for another individual.

5. Pride: the feeling of being too good for a person, place, or thing. We as individuals are better than all else, as we are gods in the flesh. Be too good for something. We are superior!

6. **Anger:** is the blinding inhibitor to which it causes most people to error. Call it the blinding factor for the majority. As unto the Satanist anger is beneficial in ritual as one of the key ingredience of desire, the emotions. Remember! There's always proper times and places. Anger is a great motivator in destruction spells.

7. **Hate:** the driving force to maintaining self-preservation and superiority. Don't be placed at the mercy of others. Hate is directed to those who would oppose us, insult us, and despise us. It's not possible to like everyone.

8. **Lust:** a thought, a desire, and fantasy. To visualize another individual naked wanting every inch of them. Visualizing very intense sexual acts with the other. There are many lust demons. The male

is called incubus and female a succubus. There is nothing wrong with going and craving after that very thing that produces life. The joys of the flesh. Indulgence is very healthy for people. Its compulsion that keeps and causes problems. The lust for life keeps life in motion.

9.  **Love:** the act of a shared feeling with family and friends. Unconditional love means loving another no matter what they have done. Going out on special occasions with your girl-friend or wife to celebrate one another's birthdays, anniversaries, and any other happy times between each other. Also, in the times when one or the other is sad, to help them through difficult moments. A candle light dinner, a walk on the beach, or a night at the movies. A soft expression to show dedication and honor to the other. Here is a short story: The sparkle in her eye as she spoke in that soft tone while she looked up at the night sky, with her eyes closed for a second I knew she was ready to go home. She had given me this warm welcoming feeling of a fire that ignited in my heart. I felt peace for that moment. Could this be an unspoken love between two people who don't even know each other? It surely must be. I felt no lust for this girl in my inner self, only I felt love for this girl so wonderful. I find myself lost for words and not enough right moments. Can and will there ever be a time or place? An opportunity for a life time of memories? This unexplainable welcoming home at the point where time stands still. Willing to give up, to

sacrifice, to have the one wonderful other that is connected to your soul. Sharing winters out in the cold with all the snow, becoming freezing cold from playing together in the snow. Going back inside the house and sitting next to the fireplace cuddling each other and feeling the warmth. Soft kisses and staring into each other's eyes communicating unspoken words of love and compassion. Touching softly noses and holding on to every second, not wanting this moment to ever end. The seasons keep changing and 50 years has passed by and still happily together. We raised wonderful children that have grown to be great in the world. We're in our nineties and the first flame of young love and compassion for each other still burns bright. Hoping we die together cuddled in bed asleep, not letting go of the first time we met. We were never rich or poor. We owned an amazing house that raised a family and a few pets. Being together meant no worries, stress, no troubles, nothing else mattered, but the joy and love together. THERE IS SO MUCH BEAUTY IN LOVE!